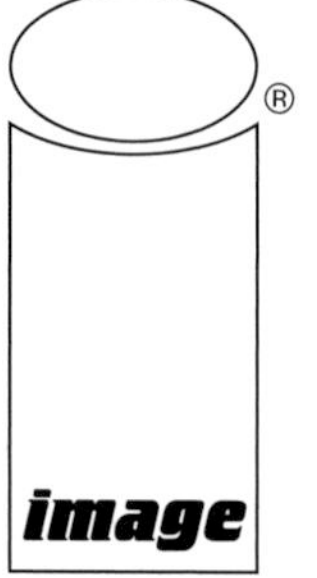

IMAGE COMICS, INC.

Robert Kirkman - chief operating officer
Erik Larsen - chief financial officer
Todd McFarlane - president
Marc Silvestri - chief executive officer
Jim Valentino - vice-president

Eric Stephenson - publisher
Ron Richards - director of business development
Jennifer de Guzman - pr & marketing director
Branwyn Bigglestone - accounts manager
Emily Miller - accounting assistant
Jamie Parreno - marketing assistant
Emilio Bautista - sales assistant
Jaemie Dudas - administrative assistant
Kevin Yuen - digital rights coordinator
Tyler Shainline - events coordinator
David Brothers - content manager
Jonathan Chan - production manager
Drew Gill - art director
Jana Cook - print manager
Monica Garcia - senior production artist
Vincent Kukua - production artist
Jenna Savage - production artist
Addison Duke - production artist

www.imagecomics.com

volume one Family

written by **GREG RUCKA**

art and letters by **MICHAEL LARK**

with STEFANO GAUDIANO & BRIAN LEVEL

colors by **SANTI ARCAS**

cover by MICHAEL LARK

publication design by MICHAEL LARK & ERIC TRAUTMANN

edited by DAVID BROTHERS

FAMILY
CHAPTER ONE

"CATALOGUE OF **TRAUMA**, AS FOLLOWS:

"BULLET ONE: VENTRAL-DORSAL TRAVERSE, ENTERING EIGHTH INTERSPACE ON RISING TRAJECTORY...
"...ROUND **FRAGMENTED**, COMPOUNDING FRACTURE OF THE RIB AT PENETRATION SIGHT.
"ROUND EXITED FOURTH INTERSPACE, RIGHT DORSAL.

"BULLETS TWO AND THREE FOLLOWING SIMILAR TRAJECTORY...

"...WITH THE SECOND PUNCTURING THE RIGHT **LUNG,** AND THE THIRD AN INTRACLAVICULAR PENETRATION WITH CORRESPONDING SCAPULAR EXIT.

"RESULT: **FULL** HYPOVOLEMIC DECOMPENSATION WITH CORRESPONDING RESPIRATORY COLLAPSE DUE TO IMPAIRED LUNG FUNCTION AND INADEQUATE PERFUSION...

"...OR, ACCORDING TO TELEMETRY, DOWN AND DYING.

"NOW, THE QUESTION:
"HOW LONG WERE YOU OUT?"

"I'M...NOT SURE...
"...A MINUTE?

"MAYBE TWO?"

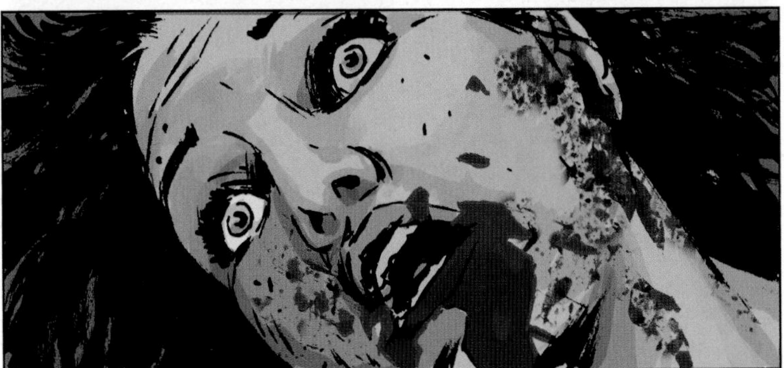

"I GET DISORIENTED, YOU KNOW THAT...
"...AND IT HURTS...
"...GOD, BUT IT ALWAYS HURTS...
"...IT'S LIKE I'M NOT IN MYSELF WHEN IT HAPPENS, LIKE I'M OUTSIDE, WATCHING MYSELF THROUGH GLASS...."
"INTERESTING. POSSIBLY A RESULT OF THE ENDORPHIN DUMP INTERACTING WITH THE FIGHT-OR-FLIGHT IPS RELEASE.
"ALL RIGHT, WHAT HAPPENED NEXT?"
"YOU KNOW WHAT HAPPENED NEXT, JAMES."
"I WANT TO HEAR IT FROM YOU, EVE...
"...I'M ASKING YOU WHAT YOU DID, WHAT YOU FELT."
"I... I DON'T LIKE TALKING ABOUT IT. I DON'T WANT TO TALK ABOUT IT...
"...PLEASE, JAMES? DON'T MAKE ME TALK ABOUT IT."
"THAT'S NOT A CHOICE, I'M AFRAID.
"I HAVE TO KNOW...

"...EVE...
"...YOUR FAMILY HAS TO KNOW."

"I KILLED THEM, JAMES.
"I KILLED ALL THREE OF THEM...

TRANSCENSOR EFFECT: HIERARCHIES
TEMPLATE
...THEY ONLY WANTED SOMETHING TO EAT.
THE FAMILY PROVIDES FOOD FOR ALL CITIZENS, AS YOU KNOW.
IF THEY'RE DOCUMENTED RESIDENTS OF THE DOMAIN, THEY RECEIVE THEIR ALLOWANCE.
THEY BROKE INTO A FAMILY RESIDENCE, FOREVER. UNUSED, YES, BUT FAMILY PROPERTY.
THEY PICKED A LOW-SECURITY LOCATION, THEY CAME ARMED, AND THEN THEY TRIED TO KILL YOU.
HAVE YOU CONSIDERED WHAT WOULD'VE HAPPENED IF YOU HADN'T BEEN THE ONE TO ENCOUNTER THEM?
IF THEY'D RUN INTO YOUR SIBLINGS?
OR, GOD FORBID, YOUR PARENTS?
WE'RE LUCKY IT WAS YOU.
MAYBE.

YOU CAN PUT YOUR SHIRT ON.
JAMES?
HMM?
DOES EVERYONE FEEL LIKE THIS?
WHEN THEY HAVE TO KILL SOMEONE, I MEAN?
I MEAN, THIS IS NORMAL, RIGHT?
TO FEEL LIKE THIS?
NO, EVE. THEY DON'T.
DON'T LET IT WORRY YOU, I'LL GIVE YOU SOMETHING TO HELP WITH IT.
WE HAVE TO FOLLOW-UP ON THE PLATELET THERAPY AFTER YOU AND JONAH FINISH UP AT HARVEST ONE.
I'LL GIVE YOU SOMETHING THEN, ALL RIGHT?
YOU WON'T TELL THEM WHAT WE TALKED ABOUT, WILL YOU, JAMES?
FATHER OR JONAH OR ANYONE?
OF COURSE NOT.
I WOULD NEVER BETRAY YOUR CONFIDENCE, I PROMISE YOU.

Central California -
The San Joaquin Valley
Facility: Harvest One
Family: Carlyle

Population [Family]: 2 (temporary)
Population [Serf]: 512
...PHYSICALLY SHE'S FINE, A FULL RECOVERY, PRECISELY AS DESIGNED...
...IT'S HER EMOTIONAL STATE THAT I'M WORRIED ABOUT...

Population [Waste]: 32,500 (estimated)
...SHE'S ASKING SOME PROBLEMATIC QUESTIONS.
AGAIN?

YOU WERE SUPPOSED TO TAKE CARE OF THAT, JAMES.
I'M INCLUDING ANOTHER OXYTOCIN BUMPER WITH THE BLOOD-SPIN...
...BUT IT NEEDS TO BE REINFORCED THIS TIME, JONAH.
IT WON'T WORK IF THERE'S NO ONE FOR HER TO BOND WITH.
SHOW HER SOME LOVE, YOU MEAN.
EXACTLY.

SIR, YOUR SISTER HAS ARRIVED.
THANK YOU.
NO TIME LIKE THE PRESENT.
I'LL DO MY PART. YOU JUST MAKE SURE THAT BUMPER DOES ITS JOB...
"...WE CAN'T HAVE HER GETTING IDEAS."
FOREVER!
CARLYLE
ODERINT DUM METUANT

I HEARD ABOUT WHAT HAPPENED AT THE GUEST HOUSE.
THANK GOD YOU'RE ALL RIGHT!
I'M FINE. I'M SO SORRY I'M LATE, JONAH...
...I HAD TO GO UP TO SEQUOIA TO SEE JAMES FOR TREATMENT.
I TRIED TO EXPLAIN YOU NEEDED ME HERE--
SHH, FOREVER, SHH, NONE OF THAT...
...I'M JUST GLAD YOU'RE OKAY.
YOU'RE SURE YOU'RE UP TO THIS?
I GO WHERE MY FAMILY NEEDS ME.
THAT'S MY SISTER.

"MISS CARLYLE - COMMANDER - I'M GLAD TO SEE YOU'RE ALL RIGHT."
"THANK YOU, SERGEANT ORIOSO. YOUR REPORT, IF YOU PLEASE?"
"YES, MA'AM.
"AT OH-THREE-TWENTY-TWO THIS MORNING, MORRAY FAMILY FORCES LAUNCHED AN ASSAULT ON THIS FACILITY.
"WE HAD NO WARNING, NOTHING PRIOR ON RADAR OR THERMAL. NO IDEA HOW THEY GOT SO CLOSE TO THE WALLS UNDETECTED.
ROMAINE
KALE
CARROTS
"THE ENTIRE GRID WENT DARK DURING THE ATTACK, THE WHOLE SECURITY NETWORK SIMPLY COLLAPSED...
"...THEY PUSHED STRAIGHT FOR THE COLD STORAGE, STRAIGHT FOR THE SEED VAULTS.
"WE BARELY STOPPED THEM IN TIME."

YOU RAN DIAGNOSTICS?
AS SOON AS WE COULD, YES, MA'AM.
THERE'S NO SIGN OF A SYSTEM FAULT.
WHICH MEANS IT WAS SHUT DOWN. NOT SABOTAGED. NOT HACKED.
WHICH IN TURN MEANS WE'VE BEEN BETRAYED.
YOU'RE JUMPING TO CONCLUSIONS, JONAH.
MA'AM, FOR-GIVE ME FOR ASKING THIS, BUT WE HEARD ABOUT WHAT HAPPENED TO YOU...
...DO YOU THINK THE ASSAULT ON YOU--
I DON'T. I WAS ATTACKED BY WASTE, NOT SOLDIERS.
WE'RE POSITIVE IT WAS MORRAY?
WE TOOK ONE ALIVE.
I WANT TO TALK TO HIM.
HER, ACTUALLY, AND YOU CAN'T.
SHE DIDN'T SURVIVE INTERROGATION.

THEY CAME FOR THE GRAIN, FOREVER, THEY PRACTICALLY WALKED IN THROUGH THE DOOR.
A DOOR ONE OF OUR PEOPLE OPENED FOR THEM.
THE ONLY PEOPLE WHO COULD'VE OPENED THE VAULT ARE SENIOR TECHNICAL STAFF.
OR ONE OF US.
YOU'RE NOT SERIOUSLY ACCUSING ONE OF OUR FAMILY?
OF COURSE NOT! I JUST DON'T WANT TO JUMP TO ANY CONCLUSIONS--
WE HAVE BEEN BETRAYED, FOREVER!
AND YOU KNOW WHAT FATHER WOULD DEMAND OF YOU IF HE WAS HERE.
WE HAVE TO SEND A MESSAGE.
YOUR SOLDIERS DIED HERE.
YOU KNOW WHAT YOU HAVE TO DO. YOU KNOW WHAT'S EXPECTED OF YOU.
SERGEANT ORIOSO, PLEASE ASSEMBLE THE SENIOR TECHNICAL STAFF IN THE COURTYARD...

"...AS WELL AS THEIR FAMILIES...."
ALL PRESENT AND ACCOUNTED FOR, MA'AM.
THANK YOU, SERGEANT.
I BEG YOU TO LISTEN TO ME CAREFULLY.
IN LIGHT OF LAST NIGHT'S ATTACK, WE HAVE... CONCLUDED THAT SOMEONE WITHIN THE FACILITY WAS IN COLLUSION WITH MORRAY FORCES.
SOMEONE WHO HAD CLEARANCE TO DISABLE THE SECURITY ON THE COLD VAULTS.
ONE OF YOU.
MY FATHER'S POLICY REGARDING BETRAYAL IS UNEQUIVOCAL ON THIS MATTER, AS YOU KNOW.
HE REQUIRES AN EXAMPLE MUST BE MADE.
A CONFESSION WILL SPARE YOUR FAMILIES AND YOUR COLLEAGUES.
BUT IF NO ONE CLAIMS RESPONSIBILITY FOR THIS... ACT OF TREASON...
...I HAVE NO CHOICE BUT TO EXECUTE ALL OF YOU TO SERVE AS A WARNING TO OTHERS.

FINE. SERGEANT, LINE THEM--
WAIT.
PLEASE.
ME...
...I DID IT, IT WAS ME.
DAD, DON'T--
YOU BE QUIET, CADY.
YOU LET THIS BE WHAT THIS WILL BE.

I DID IT, YOU UNDER-STAND? IT WAS ME.
YOU'VE DONE THE **RIGHT** THING IN COMING FORWARD.
FOREVER...

...YOU KNOW WHAT TO DO.

ONE IN THE BACK OF THE **HEAD**, I THINK...

...QUICK AND PAINLESS. OR SO I HEAR.
I'M **SORRY**, IT **ISN'T**.

I SPEAK FROM SOME **EXPERIENCE**.

SO IT'S TRUE WHAT THEY SAY ABOUT YOU? FOREVER CARLYLE? THE LAZARUS?
WELL, THEN, I SUPPOSE YOU WOULD, AT THAT.
I THINK YOU'RE LYING, SIR.
DOES IT MATTER?
OF COURSE IT MATTERS! IT MATTERS IF YOU'RE INNOCENT! IT MATTERS IF THERE'S STILL A TRAITOR IN OUR HOUSE!
WHY WOULD YOU THROW YOUR LIFE AWAY?
YOU, YOUR BROTHER, YOUR KIND, YOU TALK A LOT ABOUT FAMILY.
IF THAT WORD MEANT ANYTHING TO YOU, YOU'D KNOW THE ANSWER ALREADY.
YOUR DAUGHTER...
...I'LL TELL HER YOU LOVE HER.
TRUST ME, MISS CARLYLE...
...SHE KNOWS.

...THERE WE GO, DONE...

...YOU'LL HAVE SOME TINGLING FOR THE NEXT HOUR OR SO, NOTHING TO WORRY ABOUT.

I HEARD ABOUT THE... UNPLEASANTNESS AT HARVEST ONE.
YOU DID WHAT YOU HAD TO DO FOR YOUR FAMILY, YOU KNOW THAT, OF COURSE.
BUT IN LIGHT OF OUR TALK THIS MORNING, I HAVE TO ASK, EVE...

...HOW ARE YOU FEELING?
FINE, JAMES...

...I FEEL FINE....

CARLYLE
ODERINT DUM METUANT

FAMILY
CHAPTER TWO

Puget Sound
Family: Carlyle
FOREVER? I'VE GOT YOUR REGIMEN LAID OUT.

Population [Family]: 6 (2 permanent)
I'LL TAKE THEM LATER.
NO...

...YOU'LL TAKE THEM NOW, LITTLE SISTER.
WHAT HAVE JAMES AND I TOLD YOU ABOUT MESSING WITH YOUR MAINTENANCE SCHEDULE?
I HATE IT WHEN YOU CALL IT THAT...

...MAKES ME FEEL LIKE A MACHINE.
COME HERE, LET'S TAKE A LOOK AT YOU.

NO RESIDUAL PAIN?
NO, BETH.
PROBLEMS BREATHING? SORENESS?
NO, BETH.
PAIN IN MOTION?
NO, BETH.
42
99
100/5
80
83

DIZZINESS? ANY AURAL DISCOMFORT, TINNITUS, LIKE THAT?
NO, BETH.
09:20
GET DRESSED. PILLS ARE ON THE DRESSER.
FATHER WANTS YOU IN THE STUDY IN FIVE MINUTES FOR YOUR REPORT.

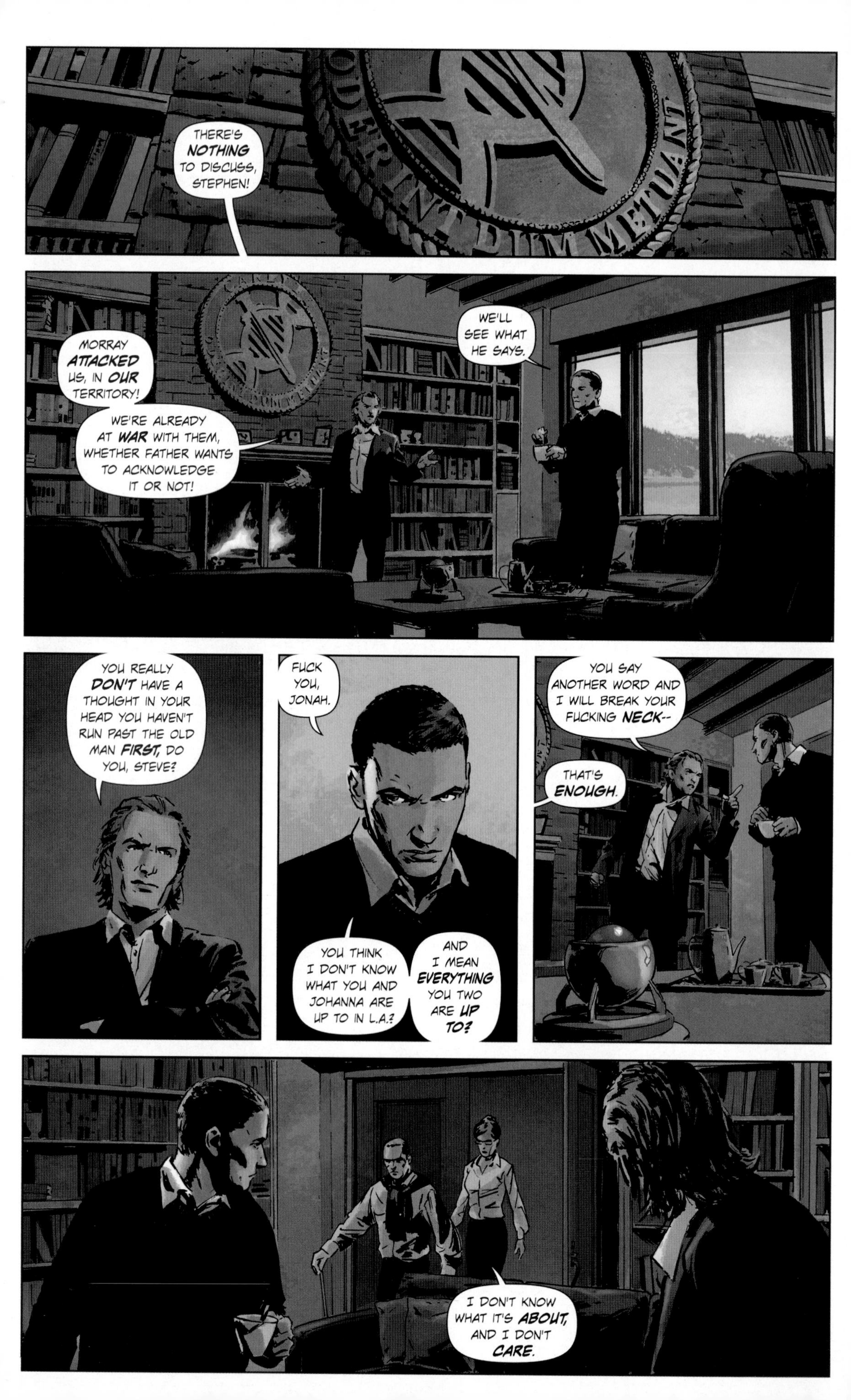
THERE'S NOTHING TO DISCUSS, STEPHEN!
MORRAY ATTACKED US, IN OUR TERRITORY!
WE'RE ALREADY AT WAR WITH THEM, WHETHER FATHER WANTS TO ACKNOWLEDGE IT OR NOT!
WE'LL SEE WHAT HE SAYS.
YOU REALLY DON'T HAVE A THOUGHT IN YOUR HEAD YOU HAVEN'T RUN PAST THE OLD MAN FIRST, DO YOU, STEVE?
FUCK YOU, JONAH.
YOU THINK I DON'T KNOW WHAT YOU AND JOHANNA ARE UP TO IN L.A.?
AND I MEAN EVERYTHING YOU TWO ARE UP TO?
YOU SAY ANOTHER WORD AND I WILL BREAK YOUR FUCKING NECK--
THAT'S ENOUGH.
I DON'T KNOW WHAT IT'S ABOUT, AND I DON'T CARE.

WE HAVE SERIOUS MATTERS TO DISCUSS, AND I WILL NOT HAVE MY SONS ACTING LIKE THEY'RE SIX INSTEAD OF SIXTY.
AM I UNDER-STOOD?
YES, SIR.
YES, SIR.
WHERE IS YOUR SISTER?
FOREVER WILL BE HERE SHORT--
NOT THE LAZARUS...
...JOHANNA. WHERE IS SHE, JONAH?
SHE... SHE THOUGHT SHE SHOULD STAY AT THE PALISADES RESIDENCE, SIR.
IN CASE MORRAY TRIED TO START ANY-THING WITH THE WASTE.
YOU TELL HER THAT THE NEXT TIME I CALL A FAMILY MEETING, IT INCLUDES HER...
...UNLESS SHE NO LONGER WISHES TO BE CARLYLE.
WHERE THE HELL IS EVE?
HERE, FATHER.
GOOD, GOOD GIRL.
ALL OF YOU, GIVE YOUR LITTLE SISTER YOUR ATTENTION.
AT OH-THREE-TWENTY-TWO HOURS YESTERDAY MORNING, A MORRAY STRIKE TEAM ASSAULTED HARVEST ONE.

THEY EVADED EARLY-WARNING SYSTEMS AND BREACHED THE COMPOUND BEFORE AN ALARM COULD BE RAISED.
SERGEANT ORIOSO MUSTERED A DEFENSE AND REPELLED THE ASSAULT. THEIR OBJECTIVE WAS THE SEED VAULTS.

CARLYLE LOSSES-- OUR LOSSES-- WERE...
...THEY WERE...

...SUBSTANTIAL....

PLEASE CONTINUE, FOREVER.
YES, SIR.
THIS MAN...

...SAMUEL ROSALES, CONFESSED TO DISABLING SECURITY AND CLAIMED HE WAS AN AGENT OF FAMILY MORRAY.

FOLLOWING HIS EXECUTION FOR TREASON, HIS BELONGINGS WERE CONFISCATED AND THE LODGINGS WHERE HE LIVED WITH HIS DAUGHTER, ONE OF THE STAFF RESEARCHERS, SEARCHED.

I CAN FIND NO EVIDENCE AS TO HOW HE WAS RECRUITED BY MORRAY, NOR HOW HE COMMUNICATED WITH THEM.

THANK YOU, FOREVER.
THOUGHTS?
WHAT DO WE KNOW ABOUT THE DAUGHTER?
CADY ROSALES. BORN EARLY '30S, TESTED IN '42, SCORED HIGH FOR TECHNICAL APTITUDE AND MEAN INTELLIGENCE.
SUBSEQUENTLY LIFTED AND SENT FOR EDUCATION AT STANFORD.
TRAINED IN BIOTECHNOLOGY, SPECIFICALLY AGRICULTURAL GENETICS...
...ASSIGNED TO HARVEST ONE LAST YEAR.
NOTHING ELSE OF NOTE, NO REPRIMANDS, NO CAUTIONS, AND NO INDICATIONS OF SUBVERSIVE LEANINGS.
STANFORD, THAT'S WHY I KNOW THE NAME....
WE BROKE OFF TRADE WITH MORRAY FIVE YEARS AGO, AND THE WORD IS THEIR HARVESTS HAVE SUFFERED EVER SINCE, AND THAT THEY'RE HAVING TROUBLE CONTROLLING THEIR WASTE.
IT'S CERTAINLY PLAUSIBLE THEY WOULD GO AFTER OUR SEEDS.
IT'S NOT PLAUSIBLE, STEVE, IT'S CERTAIN!
THEIR SOIL IS FALLOW, IT'S FUCKING DEAD WITHOUT OUR STRAINS TO GROW IN IT!
LOOK, WE KNOW WHO DID IT, WE KNOW WHY THEY DID IT. THE ONLY QUESTION IS WHAT WE'RE GOING TO DO IN RESPONSE.
AND WHAT DO YOU THINK WE SHOULD DO, JONAH?
GO TO WAR.

ALL OF YOU, LEAVE.
FOREVER, REMAIN.
YOU DON'T BELIEVE SAMUEL ROSALES' CONFESSION.
DO YOU?
NO, SIR.

YET YOU EXECUTED HIM FOR TREASON.
WHY DID YOU DO THAT?
FOREVER.
I ASKED YOU A QUESTION, YOUNG LADY.
I... I DIDN'T WANT TO...
BUT YOU DID IT, AND I WANT TO KNOW WHY.
DID IT FEEL GOOD? DID YOU LIKE IT?
DID YOU WANT TO SEE HIM BLEED?
DID IT MAKE YOU FEEL STRONG, KILLING AN UNARMED OLD MAN--
I HAD TO! TREASON MEANS DEATH, JONAH MADE ME--
--HE WAS GOING TO EXECUTE EVERYONE IF HE DIDN'T GET A CONFESSION!

OH, JONAH...
...YOU FOOLISH BOY.
FIVE CHILDREN, AND ONLY ONE OF THEM IS WORTH A DAMN.
COME HERE, EVE...
...THERE'S SOMETHING YOUR FATHER NEEDS YOU TO DO FOR YOUR FAMILY....

HOW LONG IS SHE GOING TO BE IN THERE WITH HIM?
JEALOUS?

THIS IS FAMILY BUSINESS! SHE SHOULDN'T EVEN BE IN THERE!

SHE'S NOT EVEN HIS REAL DAUGHTER, SHE'S JUST--
YOU SHUT YOUR FUCKING MOUTH, JONAH.

YOU DON'T SAY IT, YOU DON'T EVEN THINK IT ANYWHERE SHE COULD POSSIBLY HEAR.
DO YOU KNOW WHAT HAPPENS IF SHE LEARNS WHAT SHE REALLY IS? THE QUESTIONS SHE'LL START TO ASK?

SO SHE LEARNS THE TRUTH AND SHE GOES BUGFUCK CRAZY, BIG DEAL.
WE PUT HER DOWN...
...AND THEN YOU AND JAMES PLAY HIDE-THE-PIPETTE FOR A WHILE AND MAKE US ANOTHER ONE.
I'LL FUCKING KILL YOU--
nGHn

--YOU MISERABLE LITTLE ABORTION, YOU MALIGNANT PIECE OF SHIT--
ahh! AHHH!! CRAZY BITCH LET GO--
--I WILL FLAY YOU OPEN, I WILL--
--LET ME UP LET--
--DRAIN EVERY WORTHLESS DROP OF YOUR BLOOD--
BETH!!
KNOCK IT OFF!
CRAZY LITTLE--

--KEEP HER AWAY FROM ME--

WHAT DO YOU WANT?!?
I'M SORRY, SIR, YOUR MOTHER--

GET OUT!

TAKE YOUR HANDS OFF ME, STEPHEN.
I TOLD YOU TO GET OUT, YOU FETID--
FATHER WANTS TO SPEAK WITH YOU IN THE STUDY, STEPHEN.
BETHANY, HE SAYS YOU'RE FREE TO GET BACK TO YOUR WORK WITH DR. MANN, OR IF YOU'RE NEEDED AT THE UNIVERSITY, WHICHEVER YOU DESIRE.
I'M TO ACCOMPANY YOU BACK TO LOS ANGELES.
WE'RE TO LEAVE IMMEDIATELY.
WAIT, WITH ME?
DOES THIS MEAN HE'S DECIDED? WE'RE GOING TO WAR AGAINST MORRAY?
WE'RE TO LEAVE IMMEDIATELY.

Los Angeles
Family: Carlyle
Population [Family]: 3 (2 permanent)

"YOU SHOULD HAVE REPAIRED MORE AFTER THE EARTHQUAKE..."
Population [Serf]: 322,274
Population [Waste]: 2,874,500 (estimated)

...YOUR DOMAIN LOOKS LIKE A WAR ZONE, JONAH.

WE REBUILT WHAT THE FAMILY NEEDS. THERE'S NO POINT IN WASTING RESOURCES ON WASTE WHO CAN'T APPRECIATE IT.
WHAT DID YOU AND FATHER TALK ABOUT?

HE'S ASKED ME TO DO SOME-THING.
FOR OUR FAMILY.

JO?
JOHANNA?
I'M IN THE **BATH.**

DO MY BACK.

WHY IS SHE HERE, JONAH?
I DON'T KNOW, AND SHE ***WON'T*** TELL ME.

WHAT DO YOU MEAN, SHE ***WON'T?*** SHE DOESN'T HAVE A ***CHOICE***, IT'S IN HER FUCKING ***GENES*** TO DO WHAT WE ***WANT!***

FATHER MUST'VE ORDERED HER NOT TO TELL ANYONE, NOT EVEN OTHER FAMILY.
I DON'T LIKE THAT.
HE ASKED WHY YOU WEREN'T AT THE MEETING.
I TOLD HIM YOU WERE WORRIED ABOUT SECURITY FOLLOWING THE MORRAY ATTACK.
HE DIDN'T BELIEVE YOU.
NO, HE SAID YOU COULDN'T BE BOTHERED.
IF THAT'S WHAT THE OLD FOOL THINKS OF ME, FINE...
...FOREVER IS THE PROBLEM RIGHT NOW, NOT HIM.
WE'RE GOING TO NEED TO KEEP AN EYE ON HER...
...FIND OUT WHY THE LITTLE PERVERSION IS HERE, HOW MUCH SHE KNOWS. IF FATHER IS SUSPICIOUS--
SHH, JO...
...I'VE GOT MASON WATCHING HER...

"...IT'S ALL UNDER CONTROL...."

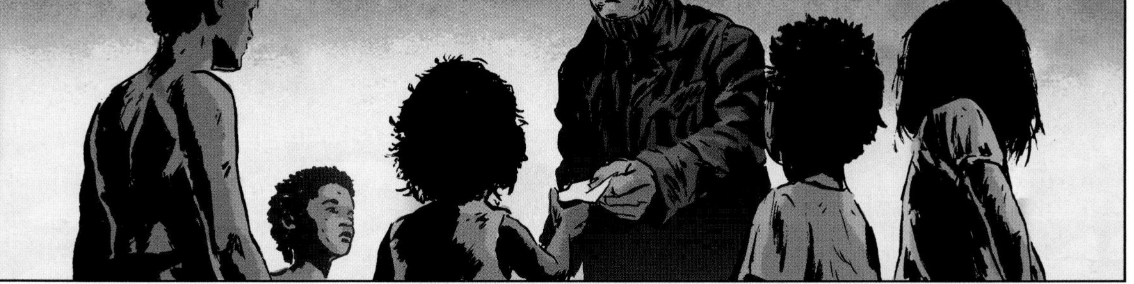

OH NO, OH NO NO NO...

...WHERE'D YOU GO, YOU BITCH?

Mason
If you keep following me,
I'm going to kill you.

Sonoran Desert, Mexico
Family: Morray

Population [Family]: 1
YOUR FATHER IS VERY STUPID, OR VERY BOLD...

Population [Serf]: 36
...TO SEND HIS LAZARUS TO US LIKE THIS.
IT DOESN'T REALLY MATTER. YOU ARE NOW A PRISONER OF FAMILY MORRAY...

...FOREVER.

CARLYLE
ODERINT DUM METUANT

FAMILY
CHAPTER THREE

Magdalena, Mexico
Family: Morray
YOU WILL SURRENDER YOUR WEAPONS AND SUBMIT TO A SEARCH.
Population [Family]: 1
I WILL NOT.
YOU WILL SURRENDER YOUR WEAPONS AND SUBMIT TO A SEARCH...
Population [Serf]: 22
Population [Waste]: 12,782
MORRAYS SE EMPACHA MIENTRAS NOSOTROS MORIMOS DE HAMBRE
...OR YOU WILL BE RESTRAINED AND WE WILL DO IT BY FORCE.
TRY IT.

<HOLD HER, AND DON'T BE GENTLE ABOUT IT-->
<MUCH AS IT WOULD AMUSE ME TO SEE THE ATTEMPT...>
<...I WOULD ADVISE AGAINST TRYING TO PLACE AN UNINVITED HAND ON MISS CARLYLE.>
<SHE IS OUR GUEST HERE, FOR NOW...>
<...AND WE WILL ACCORD HER THE COURTESY SHE IS DUE.>
<MISTER MORRAY, YOUR UNCLE'S ORDERS ARE VERY CLEAR ON THIS MATTER...>

<...THE CAPTURE OF AN IDENTIFIED ENEMY LAZARUS IS OF THE HIGHEST PRIORITY.>
<SHE IS A PRISONER, NOT A GUEST.>

HE'S ARGUING WITH ME.
YES, HE IS.

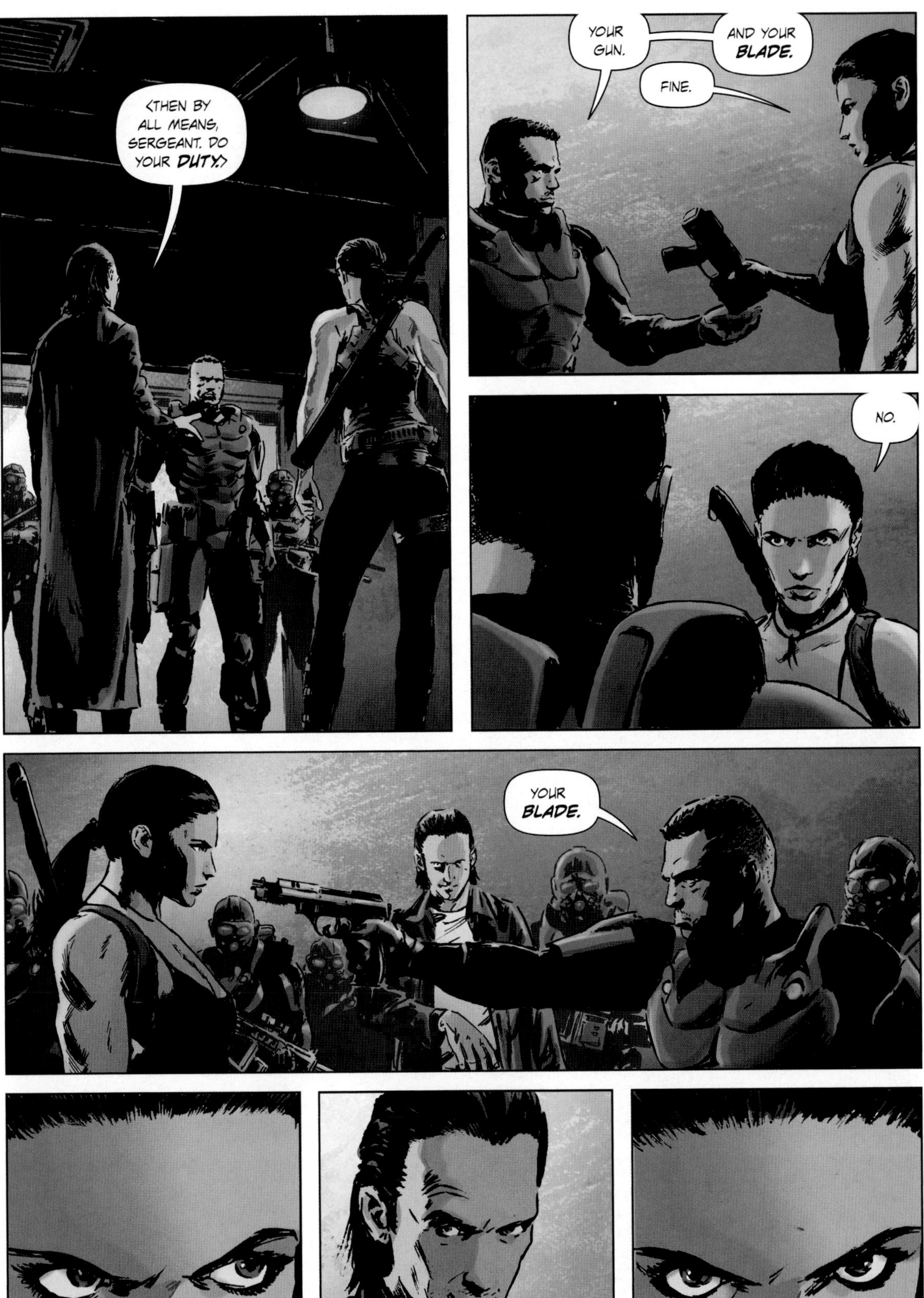
<THEN BY ALL MEANS, SERGEANT. DO YOUR **DUTY.**>
YOUR GUN.
AND YOUR **BLADE.**
FINE.
NO.
YOUR **BLADE.**

YOUR BL--
--ADE--

NO.

--AHH AHH AHH--

<--MOTHER OF GOD MY ARM OH GOD-->
<YOU ARE WASTE RAISED TO SERVICE...>

<...BUT YOU CHALLENGE MY AUTHORITY IN FRONT OF YOUR MEN?>
<I AM THE MORRAY LAZARUS. I AM THE ARM OF MY FAMILY. AND YOUR AMBITION, SERGEANT-->
<--OUTWEIGHED YOUR SENSE.>
<YOU.>
<YOU ARE NOW ELEVATED TO THE RANK OF SERGEANT.>
<GET THIS CLEANED UP, AND PREPARE FOR INSPECTION.>
<MY UNCLE WILL BE ARRIVING SOON.>

FOREVER? MIGHT I OFFER YOU SOME REFRESHMENT?
THAT WOULD BE LOVELY, THANK YOU, JOACQUIM.

Compound Sequoia
Family: Carlyle
DON'T GIVE ME THAT BULLSHIT, JAMES!
Population [Family]: 1
Population [Serf]: 24
YOU TRACK HER ALL THE TIME!
JESUS, YOU AND BETH NEVER SHUT-UP ABOUT FOREVER'S TELEMETRY AND SHIT LIKE THAT!
I DIDN'T SAY I'M NOT TRACKING HER, JONAH.
I SAID, "I CAN'T TELL YOU WHERE SHE IS."
YOU CAN'T TELL ME? YOU FUCKING WORK FOR ME!
I WORK FOR THE FAMILY, JONAH.
IT WAS MY FATHER, WASN'T IT? HE TOLD YOU NOT TO TELL ME.
I HAVE WORK TO DO--
THE OLD MAN'S NOT GOING TO BE AROUND FOREVER, JAMES.
YOU MIGHT WANT TO THINK ABOUT THAT.

CALL: MALCOLM CARLYLE.
dee-deet dee-deet dee-deet

YES, JAMES?
HELLO, SIR. I HAVE THE TELEMETRY UPDATE FOR YOU.
EVE'S BEEN TAKEN TO THE MORRAY OUTPOST IN MAGDALENA. VITALS ARE NOMINAL.
VERY GOOD.

SIR? JONAH JUST CONTACTED ME. HE WANTS TO KNOW WHERE SHE IS.
WHAT DID YOU SAY?

THAT I COULDN'T TELL HIM.
HE WASN'T HAPPY.

CONTINUE HOURLY UPDATES ON MY DAUGHTER, JAMES.
YES, SIR.

CAN YOU EAT THIS?

I ASK BECAUSE I ASSUME YOUR DIET IS RESTRICTIVE, YES?
I CAN, THANK YOU.

GUAVA?
ARE YOU HAVING ANY?

I'M NOT POISONING YOU, YOU HAVE MY WORD.
I DIDN'T THINK YOU WERE, JOACQUIM.
I CAN'T EAT THEM...

...THE ENZYMES INTERFERE WITH MY IMPLANTS.

I'M TRYING TO REMEMBER THE LAST TIME WE MET.
WHEN THE TALKS BROKE DOWN. FIVE YEARS AGO.
AH, YES. YOU WERE BARELY BIG ENOUGH TO CARRY YOUR SWORD.
I WAS FOURTEEN.
TRULY? I'D IMAGINED YOU OLDER.
I WAS VERY MATURE FOR MY AGE.
I DON'T REMEMBER YOU SAYING MUCH.
I DON'T REMEMBER YOU SAYING ANYTHING.
YES, WELL, FATHER HAD FORBIDDEN ME TO SPEAK.
MY UNCLE TOLD ME TO KILL YOU FIRST. IF THE TALKS WENT WRONG.
MY FATHER SAID SOMETHING SIMILAR ABOUT YOU.
YOU WERE THE FIRST PERSON LIKE ME I'D EVER MET.
YOU MEAN ANOTHER LAZARUS?
YES.

YOU'VE TURNED INTO A BEAUTIFUL WOMAN.
STOP.
I MEAN IT.
YOU HAVEN'T CHANGED. NOT THAT I CAN SEE.
THEY'VE PUT ME BACK TOGETHER A FEW TIMES SINCE THEN.
I THINK THEY MAKE **US** FIGHT SO **THEY** DON'T HAVE TO.
I DON'T WANT TO **FIGHT** YOU.
I DON'T WANT TO **HURT** YOU.
OUR FAMILIES DON'T UNDERSTAND.
NO.
THEY DON'T.

THAT WILL BE UNCLE.

Los Angeles
Family: Carlyle
I'M TELLING YOU HE KNOWS.

HE DOES NOT, JONAH. HE SUSPECTS.
NO, JO, HE FUCKING WELL KNOWS AND HE'S USING THE LAZARUS TO BE SURE!

SHE WAS SEEN RIDING SOUTH.
IF FATHER WAS SENDING HER TO ATTACK, SHE'D HAVE TAKEN TROOPS WITH HER.

THE ONLY REASON TO SEND HER ALONE IS TO PARLAY--
JONAH, CALM DOWN!

WE'RE ON THE BRINK OF WAR WITH MORRAY.
ALL IT WILL TAKE IS A BREATH TO KISS THE FLAMES TO LIFE.
AND YOU'RE NOT HEARING ME, JOHANNA!
HE'S SENT FOREVER WITH A BUCKET OF WATER.
THANK YOU, CHARLES.
MY HONOR, MISS JOHANNA.
YOU'RE DISMISSED.
IF FATHER SENT FOREVER TO PARLAY, HE'S CONDUCTING NEGOTIATIONS VIA BACK-CHANNEL.
FOREVER WON'T COMPROMISE FAMILY COMS. SHE CAN'T REPORT TO FATHER UNTIL SHE'S BACK IN CARLYLE TERRITORY.

SO WE KILL HER BEFORE SHE REPORTS BACK, BLAME IT ON MORRAY.
FATHER WILL HAVE NO CHOICE BUT TO DECLARE WAR.
BOOM. DONE.
I MEAN REALLY, BROTHER, IT'S NOT THAT HARD TO TRACK, IS IT?
IT WON'T WORK.
OF COURSE IT WILL WORK.
SHE'S OUR FUCKING LAZARUS, SHE CAN'T BE KILLED, REMEMBER?
OF COURSE SHE CAN. SHE DIES LIKE THEY ALL DO, IT'S WHY THEY WEAR THOSE SILLY SWORDS.
JUST MAKE THE PIECES SMALL ENOUGH AND THERE'S NOTHING LEFT TO REBUILD.
BOOM, LIKE I SAID.

WE'D HAVE TO HIT HER THE MOMENT SHE'S BACK IN OUR TERRITORY.
I'LL PUT MASON ON IT...
...MOBILIZE AN ASSAULT TEAM AND DOUBLE SURVEILLANCE ALONG THE BORDER.
A SNIPER AND A HEADSHOT COULD SOLVE ALL OUR PROBLEMS, JONAH.
AND ASK MASON TO PAY CHARLES A VISIT.
HE HEARD ENOUGH OF YOUR TANTRUM TO GUESS WHAT'S GOING ON...
...AND WE DON'T WANT THE WASTE TATTLING TO DADDY, DO WE?

I AM MORRAY. I AM THE VOICE OF MY FAMILY.
WE ARE WILLING TO HEAR YOU, MISS CARLYLE, BECAUSE WE STILL REMEMBER AND RESPECT THE ACCORDS OF MACAO. WE RESPECT YOUR FATHER, DESPITE ALL THAT HAS HAPPENED BETWEEN OUR FAMILIES.
BUT MORRAY WILL NOT BE THREATENED. MORRAY WILL NOT BE TURNED INTO ANOTHER CARLYLE DOG.
WE WILL NOT ROLL OVER FOR YOU. SO BEFORE YOU SPEAK YOUR FATHER'S MESSAGE, THIS MUST BE MADE CLEAR.
IF YOUR PRESENCE IS A CARLYLE DECLARATION OF WAR, YOU WILL CERTAINLY BE THE FIRST OF YOUR FAMILY TO DIE...
...BUT NOT, BY FAR, THE LAST.
I AM CARLYLE, MISTER MORRAY. THESE ARE THE WORDS OF MY FATHER.
HE SPEAKS, "GREETINGS, EDGAR, AND TO YOUR SON, BRIAN, AND TO YOUR RADIANT BRIDE, ANNE-MARIA, AND TO THE WHOLE OF YOUR FAMILY.
"MORRAY'S STRENGTH DOES YOU HONOR.

"BUT YOU CANNOT DINE ON STRENGTH," HE SAYS. "YOUR PEOPLE STARVE.
"UNREST IS ON THE RISE FROM DURANGO TO MEXICO CITY, AND EVEN FURTHER SOUTH.
"BY OUR PROJECTIONS, YOUR DOMAIN WILL FACE AN UPRISING BEFORE THE END OF THE YEAR.
"AT BEST, YOU WILL BE WEAKENED. AT WORST, YOUR DOMAIN WILL FALL."
MY FATHER SPEAKS, "CARLYLE OFFERS NORMALIZATION OF TRADE WITH MORRAY, GRAIN AND SEED SHIPMENTS TO RESUME IMMEDIATELY.
"IN EXCHANGE, MORRAY AGREES TO THE FOLLOWING:
"FIRST, PROMPT DELIVERY OF EIGHTEEN TARANTULA-CLASS INTERDICTORS, A SECOND SHIPMENT TO FOLLOW IN THE SAME QUANTITY WITHIN SIX MONTHS.
"MATERIEL, PARTS, AND PERSONNEL, INCLUDING INSTRUCTORS, TO BE PROVIDED. MUNITIONS EXCLUDED.
"SECOND, AND LAST," MY FATHER SPEAKS, "YOU AGREE TO IMMEDIATELY CEASE ANY AND ALL COMMUNICATION WITH OUR YOUNGEST SON, JONAH...
"...WHOSE TREACHERY IS KNOWN TO US, AS IS YOUR COLLUSION WITH HIM."
THIS IS THE CARLYLE MESSAGE TO MORRAY.
I AM TO RELAY YOUR REPLY.

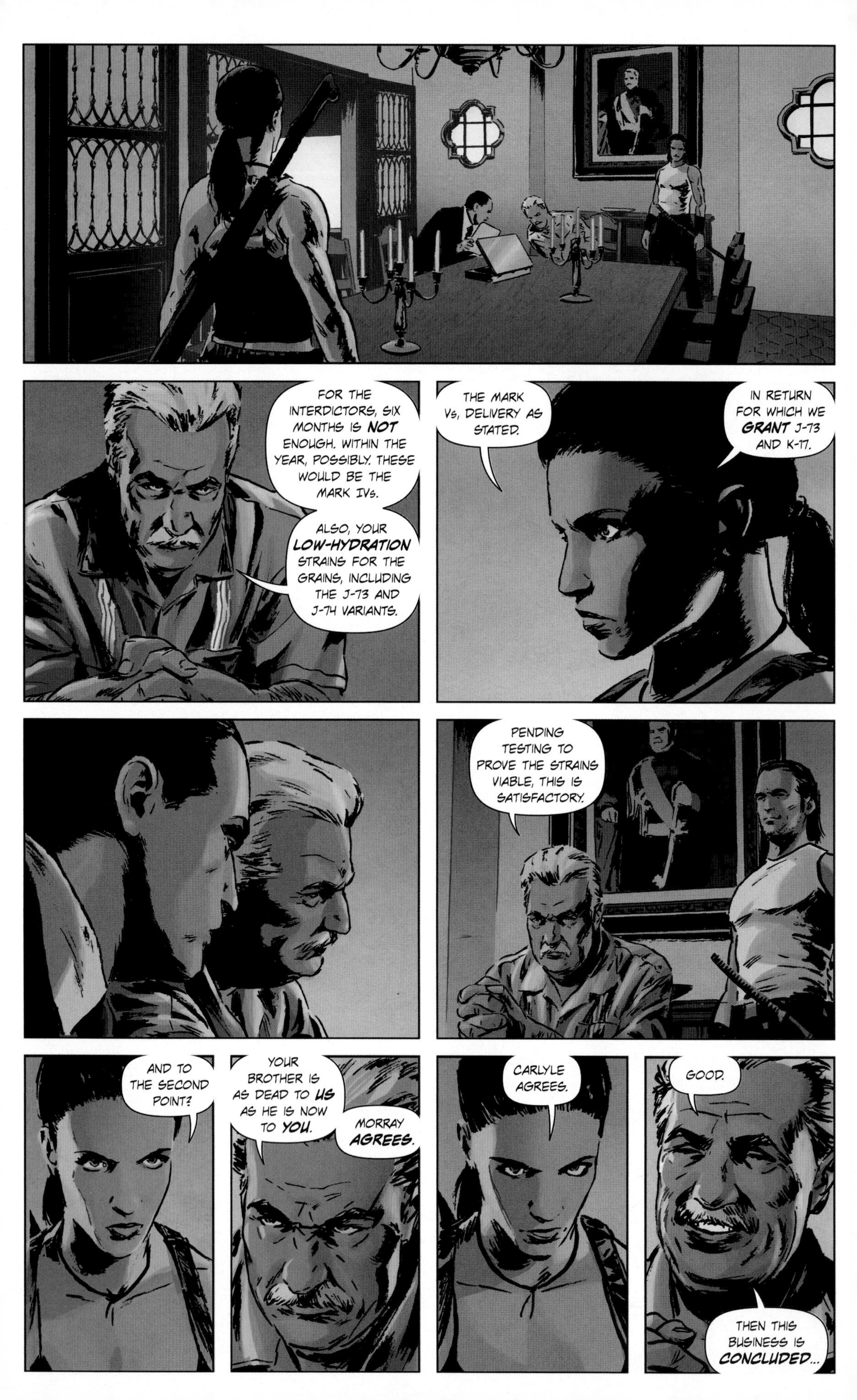
FOR THE INTERDICTORS, SIX MONTHS IS NOT ENOUGH. WITHIN THE YEAR, POSSIBLY. THESE WOULD BE THE MARK IVs.
ALSO, YOUR LOW-HYDRATION STRAINS FOR THE GRAINS, INCLUDING THE J-73 AND J-74 VARIANTS.
THE MARK Vs, DELIVERY AS STATED.
IN RETURN FOR WHICH WE GRANT J-73 AND K-17.
PENDING TESTING TO PROVE THE STRAINS VIABLE, THIS IS SATISFACTORY.
AND TO THE SECOND POINT?
YOUR BROTHER IS AS DEAD TO US AS HE IS NOW TO YOU.
MORRAY AGREES.
CARLYLE AGREES.
GOOD.
THEN THIS BUSINESS IS CONCLUDED...

...CAN WE PERSUADE YOU TO STAY FOR DINNER, MISS CARLYLE?
AT LEAST TO SHARE A DRINK WITH ME AND MY SON?
THAT IS VERY GRACIOUS OF YOU, MISTER MORRAY...
...BUT I'M SURE YOU UNDERSTAND THAT I MUST RETURN HOME AS SOON AS POSSIBLE.
OF COURSE, A PITY, BUT OF COURSE.
YOUR FATHER WILL WANT TO HEAR ABOUT THIS IN PERSON, NO DOUBT...
...YOU NEVER KNOW WHO MIGHT BE LISTENING.
LAZARUS.
YES, UNCLE?
YOU WILL SEE THE CARLYLE LAZARUS SAFELY OUT OF OUR DOMAIN.
YOU WILL LEAVE AT ONCE.
OF COURSE, UNCLE...
...IT WILL BE MY PLEASURE.

IS THERE A PROBLEM?
NO PROBLEM, NONE AT ALL...
...GPS SAYS WE HAVE JUST CROSSED INTO YOUR FAMILY'S DOMAIN.
AND SINCE IT MAY BE ANOTHER FIVE YEARS BEFORE I GET TO SEE YOU AGAIN, I THOUGHT WE MIGHT PERHAPS TAKE A MOMENT.

A MOMENT FOR WHAT?
FOR SHARING A DRINK OF WATER AND A SUNSET.

FOR SAYING GOOD-BYE.

I'D LIKE THAT.

DO YOU...?
SHHH.
I THOUGHT I HEARD...
...SOMETHI--

CARLYLE
ODERINT DUM METUANT

FAMILY
CHAPTER FOUR

Southern Sierra Nevadas
Facility: Compound Sequoia
Family: Carlyle
STILL HASN'T MOVED?
Population [Family]: 3 [2 permanent]
CARLYLE
MORRAY
NO, AND IT'S NOT DUE TO THE MORRAY JAMMING, I'VE ALREADY ACCOUNTED FOR THAT.
SHE JUST... STOPPED ABOUT THREE MINUTES AGO, RIGHT ON THE BORDER...
Population [Serf]: 28
Population [Waste]: 0
...WONDER WHY.
PERHAPS SHE'S ENJOYING THE SUNSET, JAMES.
PERHAPS YOU SHOULD, TOO.
IS THAT AN ORDER FROM THE FAMILY, BETHANY?
THINK OF IT AS FRIENDLY ADVICE, DOCTOR--
dreeetdreeetdreeetdre

dreeetdreeetdreeetdreeetdreeetdreeetdreeetdreeetdreeetdree
--TRAUMA ALERT--HER TELEMETRY'S STILL ONLINE--
VITALS CRASHING--
--SCI AT C5 AND C6, HER NECK'S BROKEN--
--DISLOCATION, LEFT SHOULDER, DISTAL RADIUS FRACTURE, LEFT WRIST--
--MULTIPLE CRACKED RIBS, PENETRATING WOUND, LEFT THIGH, MISSED THE FEMORAL--
tdreeetdreeetdreeetdreeetdreeetdreeetdreeetdreeetdreeetd
--TURN THAT FUCKING ALARM OFF!
ALL ALONG HER LEFT, COULD BE A CRASH, SHE WAS THROWN FROM THE VEHICLE--
HOW DOES SHE CRASH IF SHE'S NOT MOVING?
AN EXPLOSION? IF IT'S AN ATTACK--
--THAT DOESN'T MAKE SENSE...
I NEED TO CALL FATHER.
...WHY WOULD MORRAY ATTACK HER ON THE WAY HOME?
CARLYLE

"GOOD HIT, CONFIRM GOOD HIT..."

Los Angeles
Facility: Twins Palisades (Residence)
...VEHICLE DESTROYED.
MASON, SEND THEM IN. MAKE SURE THEY KNOW WHAT TO DO.

Family: Carlyle
Population [Family]: 2
Population [Serf]: 76
YES, SIR, MISTER CARLYLE.

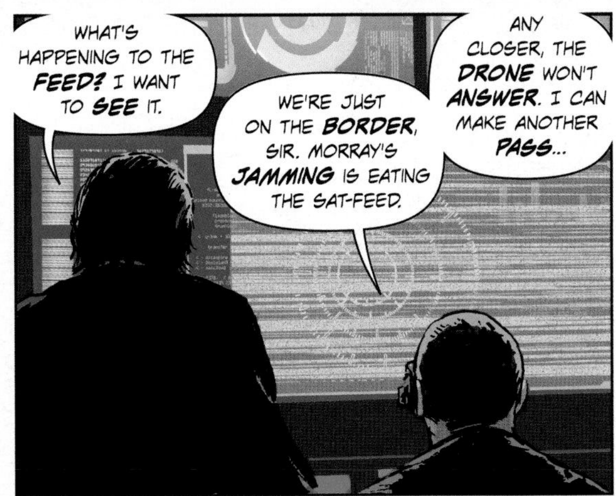
WHAT'S HAPPENING TO THE FEED? I WANT TO SEE IT.
WE'RE JUST ON THE BORDER, SIR. MORRAY'S JAMMING IS EATING THE SAT-FEED.
ANY CLOSER, THE DRONE WON'T ANSWER. I CAN MAKE ANOTHER PASS...

...BUT IT'LL TAKE A COUPLE OF MINUTES.
DO IT. I HAVE TO SEE IT...

Sonoran Desert, Mexico
Family: Morray/Carlyle Border [contested]
"...I HAVE TO BE SURE..."

khk hkkk

RIBS HAVE FUSED, SCI REGEN 97%, NERVE SIGNAL PROPAGATION RESTORED... SHE'S GOT HER EXTREMITIES BACK...
hnghh nnhhnnn--
...SHE'LL NEED TO RESET THE WRIST HERSELF BEFORE IT CAN TAKE.
SECONDARY CATECHOLAMINE RELEASE...
"...MUST BE REACTING TO SOME STIMULI..."
...SOME THREAT...
YOUR FATHER, WHAT DID HE SAY?
MHM? OH, HE SAID, AND I QUOTE...

"...FOREVER'S A BIG GIRL, SHE CAN TAKE CARE OF HERSELF."
GET HER ON HER KNEES.
...YOU'RE C-CARLYLE, YOU'RE FAMILY--
W-WAIT...
I CAN'T SEE A FUCKING THING!
I'LL CHECK THE UPLINK BANK, MAYBE WE CAN CLEAN UP THE SIGNAL.
--AHHHHNNGGHH!!!
MAKE IT QUICK!
HOLD HER.
S-STOP...

...DON'T DO THIS...
HOLD HER STILL...
JOHANNA- MISS CARLYLE, I MEAN- THE FEED WENT DOWN.
I TOLD YOU I'D TAKE CARE OF IT, MASON.
...I AM... GIVING YOU AN ORDER...
...I AM COMMANDER FOREVER CARLYLE... OF THE FAMILY CARLYLE...
NOW HIT ME.
MA'AM?
DON'T BE A PUSSY, MASON...
...TO DISOBEY ME IS TO DIE.
TO STRIKE ME IS TO DIE.
YOU WILL RELEASE ME AT ONCE...
...I'M GIVING YOU AN ORDER.

KEEP HER STI--
--LL
NOW, JOACQUIM--
AGAIN.
LIKE YOU MEAN IT.
--NNHAAAGH!

nhn
NOT EH-ENOUGH...

...IT'S GOT TO LOOK **REAL**...

"...LIKE **JONAH** DID IT..."

SON OF A--
dreeetdreeetdreeetdreetdreetdreetdreetdree
--BITCH SHE'S RED-LINING--
eeetdreeetdreeetdreetdreetdreetdreetdreetdree

--FULL FIGHT-OR-FLIGHT **RESPONSE**--

--WHAT THE **HELL** IS GOING ON DOWN THERE?

SHE'S DEFENDING HERSELF, JAMES.
LOOK AT HER SACCADIC REACTION TIME, IT'S OFF THE CHART...
...JUST BEAUTIFUL.
THE ADENOSINE BLOCKER THERAPY IS WORKING BETTER THAN I HOPED.
FOR THE LOVE OF GOD, BETHANY! SOMEONE'S TRYING TO KILL YOUR SISTER!

SHE ONLY THINKS SHE'S MY SISTER, JAMES.

COMMANDER--
--COMMANDER, **PLEASE**--

--I WAS FOLLOWING **ORDERS!!!**

...I HAVE SIGNAL, GOOD SIGNAL...

...IMAGE SHOULD BE RESOLVING NOW....

...DO YOU WANT ME TO MAKE **ANOTHER** PASS, SIR?

MISTER CARLYLE? SHOULD I MAKE ANOTHER **PASS**, SIR?

JOHANNA!
JO!

IT FAILED! IT FUCKING FAILED!
IS SHE IN THERE? LET ME THROUGH, MASON!

NO.

WH-WHAT DID YOU JUST--
--DAMMIT, MOVE!

YOUR SISTER SAYS TO TELL YOU THAT IF YOU START RUNNING RIGHT NOW...

...SHE'LL SLOW THE LAZARUS DOWN LONG ENOUGH FOR YOU TO ESCAPE.

PREP FOR TAKE-OFF.
YOU LEAVE WITHOUT ME, I WILL CARVE YOU OPEN.
YES, MA'AM.

THIS WAS NOT AN ATTACK ON MORRAY, JOACQUIM, YOU KNOW THAT, YOU KNOW MY FATHER WOULD NEVER--
OF COURSE.

PITY ABOUT THE ROVER.
YOU CAN TAKE MY BIKE.
THANK YOU.
GO WELL, FOREVER CARLYLE.
GO WELL, JOACQUIM MORRAY.

COMMANDER! THANK GOD YOU'RE--
WHERE IS HE? WHERE'S JONAH?
HE-HE'S GONE--
WHERE'S MY BROTHER?
HE'S GONE!
HE WENT AFTER YOUR SISTER, HE WENT AFTER THE LADY JOHANNA...

"...HE HURT HER, COMMANDER..."
JO?
JOHANNA, IT'S ME.
...I...I TRIED, YOU KNOW...?
...BUT I'M NOT STRONG LIKE YOU... AND HE...
...HE WOULDN'T STOP HITTING ME...
...AND THEN MASON CAME AND HE RAN....
...HE'S BETRAYED US, HASN'T HE?
HE BETRAYED THE FAMILY.
I'M AFRAID HE'LL COME BACK, FOREVER.
I'M AFRAID HE'LL HURT ME AGAIN.
NO, JO. NO.
I WON'T LET HIM.

Puget Sound
Family: Carlyle
...SHE SHOULD ARRIVE THERE BY MORNING.
SHE ASKED THAT MASON ACCOMPANY HER SINCE I COULDN'T, AND I SAID YES.
I DON'T TRUST HIM, SIR. HE WAS JONAH'S HAND FOR YEARS.
I'LL HAVE DANE KEEP AN EYE ON HIM WHEN THEY ARRIVE.
APPARENTLY MASON TOLD HER THAT JONAH HAD DEPLOYED SOLDIERS TO THE SOUTHERN BORDER.
JOHANNA WENT TO CONFRONT HIM, SHE SAYS HE PANICKED...
...WAS TALKING ABOUT KILLING ME, KILLING YOU, TAKING OVER THE FAMILY...
...HE BEAT HER PRETTY BADLY BEFORE MASON COULD STOP HIM.
I DID A PRELIMINARY SEARCH, AND ONE OF THE DRAGONS IS GONE.
HE WAS TRACKED FLYING EAST BEFORE THEY LOST THE SIGNAL.
HE'S RUNNING TO HOCK.

SHALL I PURSUE?
NOT AT PRESENT.
I'VE BEEN IN TOUCH WITH EDGAR MORRAY.
YOU DID WELL. I'M PROUD OF YOU.
THANK YOU, SIR.
NOW I WANT YOU TO HEAD BACK TO SEQUOIA, IS THAT UNDERSTOOD, YOUNG LADY?
GET SOME REST, MAKE SURE JAMES GIVES YOU A FULL EXAMINATION IN THE MORNING.
I'M GOING TO NEED YOU AT YOUR BEST IN THE COMING MONTHS, FOREVER.
YOUR FAMILY IS GOING TO NEED YOU.
YES, SIR.
GOOD NIGHT, SIR.
TRANSMISSION ENDED

Southern Sierra Nevadas
Facility: Compound Sequoia
Family: Carlyle

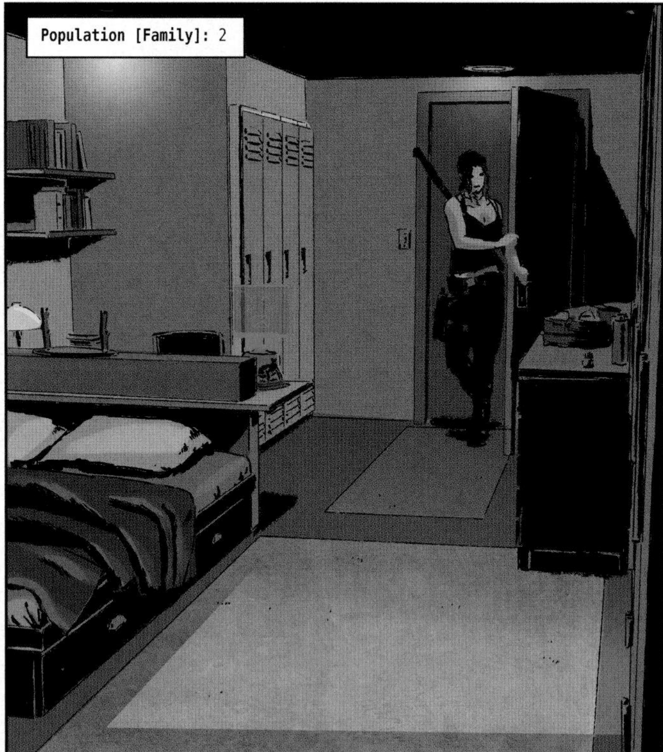
Population [Family]: 2

TO: CARLYLE_FOREVER
FROM: %#%UNKNOWN*(&%ERROR
HE IS NOT YOUR FATHER.
THIS IS NOT YOUR FAMILY

This four-page short story was written as an introduction to the world of *Lazarus*, and to illustrate the relationship between Forever and her father, Malcolm. First printed in *Previews* as part of the initial solicitation for issue 1, it was made available online as a downloadable PDF. This was the first instance of Michael, Santi, and Greg all working together.

Puget Sound
Family: Carlyle
Population (Family): 2 (permanent)
SHE'S DUE HOME SOON?
YES.
I HAVE TWO SONS AND THREE DAUGHTERS, AND ONLY ONE OF THEM IS WORTH A DAMN...

THE ONE I HAD BUILT.
THE ONE I HAD YOU BUILD FOR ME, MORE PRECISELY.

"I FIND THAT IRONIC."

DO YOU FIND THAT IRONIC, JAMES?
HONESTLY, MISTER CARLYLE? NO, I DON'T...

"...YOU AND YOUR WIFE CONCEIVED FOUR CHILDREN. THAT'S FOUR TIMES YOU THREW THE GENETIC DICE.
"YOU ASKED ME TO MAKE YOU A FIFTH, YOU TOLD ME PRECISELY WHAT YOU WANTED HER TO BE...

"...AND IN FOREVER, YOU GOT EXACTLY WHAT YOU ASKED FOR."

"IN EVERY REGARD."

YES. YES, I DID, AND YES, SHE IS.
MAY I ASK YOU A QUESTION, SIR?
YOU MAY, JAMES.

DO YOU LOVE HER?
AS HER FATHER, YOU MEAN?
YES.

SHE IS THIS FAMILY'S DEFENDER...

"...MY ARMIES ARE OUR SHIELD AGAINST OUR ENEMIES, AGAINST THE OTHER FAMILIES...
"...BUT FOREVER IS THE TIP OF MY SWORD...
"...AND LIKE THE FINEST BLADE...
"...SHE IS BEAUTIFUL...
"...AND SHE IS LETHAL...
"...AND SHE IS PRECISE...
"...AND I APPRECIATE HER FOR ALL OF THOSE THINGS.
"BUT ONE CANNOT LOVE AN OBJECT AS ONE LOVES A PERSON, JAMES.
"ONE DOES NOT LOVE A PET THE WAY ONE LOVES A CHILD.

SHE BELIEVES I LOVE HER AS A FATHER. LIKE ANY DAUGHTER, SHE CRAVES THAT LOVE.
THAT IS HOW I CONTROL HER. THAT IS ENOUGH.
SHE'S HOME.
LEAVE US.
IT'S DONE?
YES, FATHER. THE FIRE WILL BURN FOR WEEKS...
...EXACTLY AS YOU WISHED.
GOOD GIRL.
IT'S ALMOST TIME FOR DINNER.
YOU KNOW HOW YOUR MOTHER HATES IT WHEN WE'RE LATE.
YES, FATHER.

CARLYLE
ODERINT DUM METUANT